# A Bag Full of Eyes

a novella

by Robert J. Krog

# A Bag Full Of Eyes
## by Robert J. Krog

*A Bag Full Of Eyes* is a work of fiction. Names, characters, places, and incidents are products of the author's imagination. Any resemblance to actual events or persons, living or dead, is entirely coincidental.

Story copyright owned by Robert J. Krog

Cover illustration "A Bag Full Of Eyes" © 2012 by Teresa Tunaley

Cover design by Atomic Fly Studios

First Printing, January 2012

Sam's Dot Publishing
P.O. Box 782
Cedar Rapids, Iowa, 52406-0782 USA
e-mail: sdpshowcase@yahoo.com

Visit www.samsdotpublishing.com for online science fiction, fantasy, horror, scifaiku, and more. While you are there, visit the Sam's Dot Publishing Bookstore at http://sdpbookstore.com for paperbacks, magazines, and chapbooks. **Support the small, independent press...**

Ad Majorem Dei Gloriam

To Dev, Jimmy, Chris, Sean, Aaron, Mike, and Kelli.

# Acknowledgements

Thanks are due to my wife Ana, to the members of Imagicopter including but not limited to H. David Blalock, Herika Raymer, Tyree Campbell, and Jennifer Mulvihill, and to Alexis Lott. Thank you.

# A Bag Full Of Eyes

# Chapter 1

It was not until mid-afternoon that the eye-man arrived at the scene of the murders. He rode up the blood-stained, dirt track that zigzagged up the hill into the village in a two-wheeled cart pulled by a slow, lanky pony. Royal Inspector Sir Gordon stopped him just outside the gate, making sure to keep his sword in the other man's sight and to display the insignia of rank and the crucifix embroidered into his surcoat.

"You the eye-man?" Gordon asked the somewhat aged looking fellow.

"I am Victor, the eye-man, yes. Where is the corpse?"

"I'm Royal Inspector Sir Gordon. There are five corpses. The villagers pulled them up beside the wall here. They were found downhill a ways. You can park your cart on the other side of the gateway."

Victor, the eye-man, glanced past the vigorous, younger man's dark-haired head over to where the corpses were lined up, covered by canvas sheets, then clucked at his pony and flicked the reins, easing the cart over to a level patch beside the gateway. He set the brake and stepped down from the cart, standing tall and spare. Gordon observed that the man and the pony uncannily resembled one another. He was a stocky man himself, which was fine, since that fitted well his idea of how a man should appear.

Victor walked over and looked at the five corpses lined up before the village wall. He removed his hat and made the sign of the cross. Gordon had already prayed for the repose of their souls earlier with their families, but he removed his hat respectfully and waited until Victor was done. The eye-man finished praying shortly, ending with, "Eternal rest grant unto them, o Lord, and may perpetual light shine upon them." He went to the back of his cart, from which he hauled off of a medium-size, iron-bound box. Staggering under its weight, he came bowlegged toward the spot where the bodies lay, stumbling, and nearly tripping over the hem of his flapping, brown cloak. Gordon shook his head but gave the gangly fellow a hand with one end of the box. In his estimation, it was not heavy, and, in his opinion, a man should be able to carry the tools of his trade without so much effort. Such a minimal level of fitness wasn't as high on his list of important characteristics as piety, but it was high.

"Here," Victor indicated a level spot in the grass beside the corpses. They set the box down and Victor took a moment to stop huffing and puffing. He cleaned his spectacles on his tunic before proceeding. Calmly, his breathing returning to normal, he took a large key out of a pocket in his cloak and unlocked the box.

"It's a very specialized trade," he explained, taking his brass eye extractor out of his toolbox, and holding it up, carefully calibrating the adjusting screws that managed the tension between the grabber claw and the spoon.

"So I was given to understand," said Gordon, "I was told that you are the only one who does this." He was trying to be patient, but the man had taken nearly half the day to arrive, and waiting around, guarding the corpses of the five, blood-drained peasants had made him irritable.

"I'm the only one with the necessary equipment and

skills," Victor said, holding the brass instrument up a little higher in the sunlight. His spectacles cast a glare, making his brown eyes look blood-red behind them. "The skills are just as important as the equipment," he continued, "A damaged eyeball will yield little or no insight."

"Tell me about that," Gordon prompted, "What will they show?"

Victor was taking his time. He carefully set the extractor on a handkerchief beside the head of the first victim, uncovered the victim, a middle aged man with graying hair, and went back to his box. From it, he pulled a white cloth about three feet square and took it back over to the first victim. As a knight and now an inspector for a king, Gordon was used to his questions being answered rather promptly, but Victor went about his work in a rather businesslike way, paying attention to him only when he felt he had enough to spare.

"Could I get you to lift this one's head?" he asked, favoring Gordon with a brief glance over the tops of his spectacles.

Gordon grunted once, came over, and lifted the man's head. Victor carefully laid the square of cloth out underneath. He went back to his toolbox and took out a second square of cloth. As he carefully unfolded it, he explained, "Depending on the quality of the life, and of the death experience itself, you may see just the last few seconds of the victim's life, or you may see the entirety of his last day. If the victim had some powerful regret or something left undone, or just something or someone unusually important on his mind you may see that overlaying what he last saw. Once, an inspector saw

9

nothing at all. Apparently, the victim was in such terror that he completely blacked out and didn't know what happened to him."

Gordon interjected, "I was assured that this was a flawless method of discovering the murderer."

"Well," Victor answered calmly, gesturing for him to lift the head of the second victim, who was a fair-faced young man, barely more than a boy, "One does have a certain reputation, but it is a bit exaggerated."

"Exaggerated?"

"My good, man – you may set his head down – just think on it. Aside from the rare example of sheer terror erasing sight, what if the victim was hit from behind? All that is seen then is the ground coming up, or the horizon spinning. It is no flawless method, but it yields useful information more often than not."

"I see," Gordon said, trying not to let his disappointment show, "how does it work?"

"The procedure is not terribly complicated, though it can be excruciatingly painful to the recipient of the eyes." Victor regarded him directly.

Gordon frowned but said nothing, not wanting to make any assumptions.

Victor continued, "I extract the eyes of the dead men with this." He held up the eye-extractor. "I place them in this bag which preserves them, so long as they have not already begun to putrefy." He held up a small bag that was sewn together of fibers that had a metallic, golden sheen to them. "The inner lining of the bag is inscribed with the spell that causes the last vision of the eyes enclosed to be replayed when the eyes connect again to a head. I give the brave volunteer who is to receive the eyes of the dead men a potion that deadens his senses. I then take my eye-extractor and remove his eyes."

Gordon gulped at the thought, noting that the eye-man seemed to have no assistant.

Victor continued, calmly, "I place those eyes in this magical bag," he held up a bag sewn of silver fibers, "which merely preserves perfectly whatever is placed inside it. Using this instrument," – he held up another brass contraption, this one shaped like a pair of tongs but with a sort of plunger in the middle of it that appeared to be run out with a screw – "I gently put the eyes into the empty sockets, and they connect properly to the head by virtue of this spell, inscribed upon the eye-connector. Once connected, the eyes from the first bag show the recipient the last vision they beheld, and the recipient knows as much as the eyes saw. It takes approximately as much time to absorb the vision as it did to live it. When all is learned, the foreign eyes are removed, and the original eyes of the volunteer are then returned to him. That is how it is done."

"Who is the brave volunteer?" asked Gordon, trying not to show his anxiety over the question.

"Not I, if that is what you mean," said Victor, smiling, "A surgeon cannot operate upon himself. No, I had assumed it would be you, since you are the one who summoned me."

"I didn't know," admitted Gordon, "or I might not have asked for you."

"You are new in the king's service I take it?"

"I'm a vampire hunter and a very successful one,

having destroyed two of them on my own and participated in the destruction of three others. The ones in my land have fled, and I've pursued them to your land. The king was gracious enough to accept my services to rid his land of the monsters. We have no eye-man where I come from. I'd never even heard of such a thing."

"Ah, well, we could ask for another to help out, but it is not the sort of thing for which I have ever had much luck. Besides, being an inspector, no doubt you wish to review the evidence firsthand, if possible."

Gordon laughed, "Ordinarily, I wouldn't be concerned about this. The bites on their wrists and necks are all that I need to know that these were vampire slain." He gestured at the corpses, "I asked for you, because I need to know which vampire in particular I'm hunting. If it is the one I have hunted but never caught, I'll need to change my strategy."

"Ah," Victor nodded, "the one that got away."

"He's the reason I'm here."

"Is it personal then? He has offended you or wounded you in a way that cannot be forgiven?"

Gordon shook his head and gave him a quizzical look, "Isn't it enough that he's a murderer who escapes justice?"

"He has not slain a member of your family or bitten you or killed the woman you loved?"

Gordon said, "No, he's just a monster that needs to be stopped. It's a matter of principle, no more, no less. Come, let's get on with it while the sun is still shining."

They went to work, placing the corpses just as Victor needed them, setting it up so he could work swiftly and neatly on each in turn. They were two more adult men and an elderly woman. Victor gave a sad shake of his head at that and commented on the inhumanity of striking down the defenseless. As they walked away from that last corpse to get the eye-extractor and begin the gruesome part of the work, Gordon added the question, "Were you wanting a more romantic kind of story?"

"Well, you must admit that the mere pursuit of justice is much more prosaic than the pursuit of revenge on behalf of some personal injury."

Shaking his head, Gordon suggested, "Would it add poetry to the story for you if I said that I wanted to avenge his many victims, that I've memorized all of their faces though I knew them not and sworn an oath over each of their graves?"

"Why yes," smiled his bespectacled companion, hefting his eye-extractor in hand and turning to the first corpse, "Yes," he said, placing the extractor on the dead man's left eye-socket most carefully, "That would make for a better story."

Gordon turned away quickly, deeming it unnecessary to see the actual procedure. When he heard a wet, sucking sound, followed by a slight pop, he shuddered and walked away a bit. He didn't have to wait very long. Once he got to work, Victor was very efficient, and he filled the golden bag with eyes expeditiously. They carefully removed the cloths from under each head and Victor folded them neatly and placed them in his toolbox. He locked it up, and they carried it back to his cart. A question occurred to Gordon that he couldn't help but ask.

"My good fellow," he asked, "You have five pairs of

eyes in one bag. How will you tell one pair from another?"

"That's easily done. I tie the roots together with differently colored ribbons."

"Oh, I didn't know that eyes have roots."

"Of course they have roots. How else would they attach to your brains?"

"Right," Gordon said. Well, he had asked, he decided.

"The volunteer, I take it, is you?" Victor inquired, coming straight to the unpleasant point that Gordon was putting off as long as he could.

"I don't know anyone else who would recognize the monster I seek," he muttered, disgustedly.

"Begging your pardon, sir, I didn't catch your response."

He gave the eye-man a long look. "Yes," he said finally, "I'm the one."

"Then you should accompany me back to my home. I have accommodations suitable for the procedure. Will you be paying directly, or will I be sending a bill to the capital?"

"I have little need of money in general. The king's chamberlain will pay the bill."

Victor smiled warmly in response to that.

# Chapter 2

Gordon's horse was in the village stable. He fetched it quickly, turned the corpses over to the villagers with a promise to make them whole again, and fell in beside Victor, whose pony was already pulling him along the rutted road away from the village.

"Tell me, sir," Victor asked him, "who were the simple folk that the vampire slew?"

"They were simple folk, as you say, peasants, revelers returning from a wedding in another village. They left late in the afternoon and didn't live to see the dawn. The first fellow, the middle aged man, was Ponto, a farmer. The old woman was his mother, a farmer's wife. Her name was Umma. The boy, Jack, was the potter's son, but also the nephew of the man getting married. The other two men were brothers and merchants, Robert and Christopher. They'd probably never given offense that they didn't regret. They were probably as good and likable as anyone else you'd ever meet. That's why they were slain, because they were good. Now they'll have to be buried, decapitated, with holy wafers stuffed in their mouths."

"It's a grim business of which we are a part, Sir Gordon," Victor observed.

Gordon looked across at the bony man bouncing along in the cart beside him. He was as solemn as an undertaker.

"A grim business it is."

"Tell me about your quarry," suggested Victor.

"I suppose that'll pass the time as well as it may," he

said.

"If you don't want to. . ."

"No," Gordon said, "It's fine. Why not? The vampire I seek was a cooper in life, just a simple maker of barrels. Who would have thought that such an occupation could breed such cunning? He's adept at striking fast, slaughtering many, and hiding where none can easily track him down. They can't come out at day, of course, because sunlight destroys them utterly, and they have to sleep in the dark during that time. I think they would rule the world, if they weren't powerless for half their existence. They're stronger and faster than the living, but God has given us weapons against them. They've lost their souls, so they cast neither shadow nor reflection. It's easy to spot them for that reason, and because they are pale as ghosts before they feast and bloated red with blood after. One can identify them by their teeth - the canines are longer - and by their clawed fingers. A freshly cut stake of oak or ash will immobilize a vampire, if it pierces his heart, but a sword or spear thrust won't bother him, unless he has been staked, but then only if the blow is to his neck. You can cut off a vampire's head if he's been staked through the heart, you know. Running water will dissolve a vampire. They can't set foot in it or on holy ground. Stagnant water is fine for them. They recoil from symbols of the Lord. Crucifixes keep them at bay. They cannot enter the house of a believer unless they are invited in, but once they are invited, they can enter anytime they want until exorcised.

"They have powers though. They can mesmerize and hypnotize with their eyes and voice. They can change

16

their shapes to those of animals. I once found one disguised as a pig, but it was a pig that cast no shadow."

"Yes, I know the legends, Sir Gordon. Tell me about the one that you hunt."

"Sorry. The one I hunt is known for killing folks who are believers. He always strikes a priest, or a deacon, an alter boy or a nun. Or, if he cannot find one such as that, then he will kill a person leaving a church or attending a wedding or funeral. If two people are walking down a street at night and hear a frightening noise, and one invokes the name of the Lord or makes the sign of the cross to give himself courage, that is the one he will strike. He hates God."

"A terrible monster."

"Indeed. It only takes one person to actually satisfy the thirst of any vampire, but this one kills more than he has to. He never completely drains any one victim so he won't be sated until he has drunk from several, but he makes sure that the wounds are bad enough that they all bleed out and die."

"What is his name?"

"He was called Dudley."

It took them the rest of the afternoon to reach Victor's home in a small town down the way from where the five peasants had been slain. They arrived at dusk and took his pony and cart and Gordon's horse to the stable then Gordon expediently carried the box into Victor's entry hall by himself. As he turned to ask where to set it, he saw Victor standing on his stoop holding the silver bag open to the last rays of sunset.

"What are doing?" he asked.

"This bag perfectly preserves whatever is placed inside it. I may desire sunlight rather than candlelight later this evening, and by opening the bag only a little, I can let out a ray of light that will illuminate my work for several minutes."

Amazed, Gordon exclaimed, "You can't keep sunlight in a bag."

"You can keep it in this bag," insisted Victor.

"Won't it get out when you put my eyes in it for safe keeping in just a little while?"

"I shall stuff your eyes into it very quickly."

"I see."

"And you shall see many things your eyes have never beheld before this night is through."

"Right. Where do you want this box?"

"I have a special room at the end of the hall on the left. Take it in there."

There was a special chair in the room. It looked comfortable, but its purpose was clear to Gordon, for it had straps that could be cinched up to hold a man's arms and legs and head quite still. He stopped in the doorway, staring at that chair. It would be well lit by the many candles set around it on tall stands and in sconces lining the walls. There was only one window, facing east, and an instrument table beside the chair. There were also several, comfortable looking arm chairs. Behind him, Victor paused, saying, "Go in, go in, there is nothing to fear. You'll feel very little after I pour that potion into you. You'll be sore for several days after, but during the procedure, you won't feel much at all."

"It's just ghastly to contemplate," Gordon said.

18

"Then don't contemplate it, my good man. Would you like something to eat or drink before we begin?"

"No. I don't believe I have any appetite."

"Well, my father always told me, the sooner, the better. Set my toolbox on that bench."

"We might as well get it over with," Gordon agreed.

"Have a seat. I must send my maid out to find my assistant. I'll be back in just a moment."

Nervously, Gordon set his pack on the floor near the door then removed his sword, surcoat, chain mail, and boots before he sat in the chair. Poking his head back in the doorway, Victor regarded him curiously and asked, "Are you sure you aren't hungry or thirsty?"

"Quite."

Victor left again and Gordon heard him conversing with his maid. As Victor returned, she passed by in the hall. "I'm locking up as I go," she announced, "remember to leave that door open so you hear Tucker knocking at the front. I'll be gone until you finish up."

"I hear you, my dear girl," Victor called after her. To Gordon he said, apologetically, "Sue is squeamish. She's an excellent maid and a fair cook, but she won't even stay in the house when I do my work for the king. That's why I have to have Tucker here. We'll start without him, but he'll be along presently and will help immensely. His handwriting is much neater than mine. He's young, but well trained as a scribe."

"What's that got to do with anything?"

"Why of course, I've forgotten to mention part of the service that I provide. You may feel free to tell us what you witness, and he will write it down so that you have it on parchment as well as in your head."

"That might help, I think," said Gordon, approvingly.

Victor left the door open and crossed the room to a cabinet. He opened it, and Gordon saw that it was full of tightly stopped up jars and several, colorful, ceramic mugs.

"Do you have a favorite color, Sir Gordon," Victor asked him, gaily.

He shrugged, "Blue, I suppose."

"Blue it shall be," Victor announced, snatching down a jar and the blue mug. He shook the jar vigorously, pulled the cork with his teeth, and poured a muddy-looking mixture into the mug. He crossed to Gordon and said with a reassuring smile, "This is Victor's Numbing Potion, from my own, secret recipe, the last and best of my latest batch. You're lucky I have it on hand. Drink up, it'll be a great help."

"Before we get started," Gordon asked, "have you ever made a mistake, lost or destroyed someone's eyes?"

"No, never," Victor told him, "here, drink up. Like my father always said, the sooner, the better."

Gordon took a deep breath, then gulped the mixture down. It was plain tasting, neither sour nor sweet, almost flavorless, but it soon filled him with warm contentment which was followed swiftly by numbness. His mind was still clear, but he couldn't feel much of anything. He only realized after the fact that Victor had secured him to the chair.

"You won't be able to talk until I rub your mouth and jaws with this ointment," Victor explained, showing him a tiny, mother-of-pearl pot.

20

Gordon tried to nod but found that he could not.

"Is now a good time for me to confess that I'm color blind?" Victor asked him, looking down at him with the eye extractor in his hands.

"Not really," Gordon tried to say, but his tongue and lips just didn't work. He also couldn't seem to blink, but it didn't matter, because he couldn't feel his eyes either.

"Just kidding!" Victor announced happily.

He started lining the extractor up with Gordon's right eye.

"Oh, and I've only had one volunteer go blind."

Gordon found his total lack of motor control to be very frustrating. He had a very good view of the wicked-looking brass claw and spoon resting against his right eye socket

Victor snatched the extractor away and announced again, "Just kidding! Really, I'm very good at this. The first time went like a charm, so this second time should be just as easy." He set the extractor back over Gordon's right eye again. "Just kidding!" he cried joyously as he plunged the extractor into Gordon's eye socket. Gordon desperately wanted to close his eye, but a second later, it didn't matter. With his left eye, he saw Victor gently pull his right eye out of his head and place it quickly somewhere just out of the range of his remaining vision.

"This is usually where the volunteer begins to panic, but I've got something that'll calm you down just wonderfully. If you're feeling panicky, just blink, and I'll get it."

Panic didn't really describe it, but of course, Gordon could not blink. He couldn't even wink.

"Feeling calm?" Victor asked solicitously, "Your fortitude is admirable. Well, here goes nothing."

He set the extractor against Gordon's left eye socket carefully then pulled it away again. He examined the edges of the claw and spoon. He looked at Gordon and asked, "Do you have a file or hone handy? This implement is looking a little dull, and I'd like to sharpen it."

Gordon promised himself he'd kill this man as soon as he could move again.

"Just kidding," laughed Victor, "really, I keep all my equipment in tip-top shape. I have a half-wit come in and wash and sharpen everything every other year or so."

He set the extractor to Gordon's left eye again and, after a carefully measured moment, thrust it in. Gordon could see nothing, and he strained his hearing trying to figure out what was going on.

"It'll only be moment, Sir Gordon," Victor promised, "I'm just cleaning around your eye sockets. There. Done. I have that bag right here. I should have asked you if you had a preference as to which victim's last vision to view first."

There was a skipping sound, as of someone dancing.

Victor said, "I do hope you forgive me my little jokes, but I just can't help myself, because they're so unique, after all. Who else ever gets to say them? Where else would you ever hear them? Ah, here we go. The pair tied up with the yellow ribbon is for the poor, murdered, old woman. Umma, you said?"

Victor hummed happily, tunefully and there was the sound again of shuffling, dancing feet. "Here we go. I'm

22

rubbing onto your mouth and jaws the ointment that will enable you talk. There, there. Done. Just a moment, now I'm placing the eye connector against your left eye socket. Once this eye is in, you'll be able to see again, but only dimly, because your vision will be overlaid with another, more imperative one, the last moments, or even hours of the victim's life.

"You may begin to see the memories with the one eye before the second is in place, so pay attention. Sometimes they don't sync up right away, and it can be confusing. This won't work a second time, so you have to be ready. I'll get the other eye in place in a heartbeat."

# Chapter 3

Suddenly, Gordon could see again. The eye connector was pulled away, and there was Victor's skinny, old, smiling face and lanky form. Victor went rapidly at his work and was over Gordon's right eye socket as expeditiously as Gordon could have wanted, but he was paying little attention to that.

The memories of the elderly woman were already playing before his, no her, eye. In the heartbeat or several that it took Victor to put the other eye in place, Gordon saw a wrinkled hand extending out of a dress that appeared to be covering his arm and shoulder. The hand was resting on someone's arm. It was confusing at first, but he tried to focus on the memory and not on what was actually in front of him. Then, the second eye was in place, and he was seeing three things at once instead of just two. That made it far worse. He wanted to shut his eyes and shake his head, but, of course, that was impossible. He swore and swore in voiceless frustration. No! He actually heard his own voice giving vent in very foul oaths. He stifled them. A knight shouldn't speak so.

Victor's smiling face overwhelmed all for a moment as he placed a clean, white cloth over Gordon's eyes. "This will help you see only what you need to see," he explained, and, suddenly, Gordon was grateful to him.

It took a bit for the visions to correspond, but they did do so. Umma was walking down the dirt road away from her village, relying on the arm of the middle aged man, her son, who lay now at the beginning of the row of corpses of which she was the end. They walked together

24

down the road behind a large group of villagers. Some of the folk appeared to be singing. Gordon guessed it was early afternoon.

Victor's voice intruded on the vision. "Sir Gordon, what do you see?"

"She's walking away from the village with Ponto. It's still afternoon. I guess they're going to the wedding."

"Ah, this will be a long one, I think."

"I hope I don't have to attend this wedding five times."

"That is possible, but unlikely. Alert me when you want me to begin recording events."

"That I will. Could I have that drink now?"

"Of course, my good man."

He heard Victor rise from his chair and leave the room, his footsteps receding into the interior of the house.

Gordon watched, bored, as Umma fell farther and farther behind the rest of the reveling wedding goers. Eventually, she and her son passed a dirt path off the road that led away into a wooded area. She stopped him there, gesturing away down the path. He shook his head, his mouth clearly saying "No." They argued a bit, it seemed. She waggled a wrinkled finger at him some. Eventually, she snatched her hand away from his supporting arm and moved away from him. By the way her vision bounced about, he surmised that she was tottering. Ponto stepped forward to follow, but she waved him off. It seemed that he offered to go with her, calling perhaps, "Mother!" but she, again, waved him off and tottered on down that path.

Gordon heard Victor return to the room as the old woman hobbled on under the trees.

"I'm back, Sir Gordon. I found a bottle of wine that should be from a superior pressing if the other bottles of it are any means of ascertaining. Your goblet is full."

"Thank you, Victor. The vision here is becoming perplexing. Umma left the road and struck off on her own path into a wooded area."

"That's a bit odd, I suppose," agreed Victor, "Are you ready for the drink?"

"Indeed."

As Victor set the cup to his lips, Gordon watched Umma look this way and that under the trees, which swayed a little now and then in the breeze. He guessed that she was afraid of what might be out there, now that she was alone. He drank what Victor skillfully poured into his mouth and felt the better for it. It was a good wine with a refreshing taste.

"Good?" Victor asked.

"Very much so. Thank you."

In time, Umma came to a cottage in the woods, a well-appointed, little house with brick walls and a door painted red. Its roof was tiled with slate, and its windows were glass. There was a flower garden in front of the cottage, and she had to follow an out of the way path to come to the door. As she passed a window, coming up alongside the house toward the door, she saw her reflection, and Gordon started, unnerved by the fact that his eyes saw the face of Umma instead of his own. He'd known, of course, but it was still bizarre.

She raised her wrinkled, old hands, to her wrinkled, old face, grimacing at her own reflection in the glass. She ran her hands over her brow and down her nose, over her lips and pointed chin. It was her hair she lingered over the longest, though. It was totally white and what color it had been in her youth, Gordon could not tell. The people of his own land were mostly blond, his dark hair being rather out of the ordinary, but the people of this land were a mixture with blonds, browns, auburns, and black haired folk.

Finally, Umma let her hands fall, seemed to sigh, wrapped her shawl more tightly about herself, and approached that blood-red door. She hesitated before it, looking at the heavy, iron door knocker shaped in the face of a lion with a ring in its mouth. The bottom curve of the ring had a hammer head on it. The plate against which the hammer was set to strike was engraved with a smiling face from which shot out boldly, rays as of sunshine. Finally, after looking for a bit at her plain, gray dress and worn, tan shoes, she seized the knocker and struck it three times against that plate.

To his surprise, the face on the plate winced each time it was struck, then appeared to be laughing for several heartbeats afterwards. Umma backed up from the door at that point, staring at that plate. The lion from whose mouth the knocker was suspended seemed to snarl at her.

Gordon's curiosity was suddenly burning. Quickly, he related the event to Victor.

"Really?" Victor asked, his voice sounding amazed.

"I'm not making it up," Gordon insisted.

"I would never suggest that you were. That is surely the house of the witch, Nonni."

"What is this peasant woman doing at a witch's house? Peasants fear magic."

27

"But, they are also a very superstitious lot, and sometimes seek magical aid, nevertheless, Sir Gordon."

"But, it's forbidden to traffic with witches."

"But, what peasant can afford the services of a legally sanctioned magician?"

"Well, witches are an unsavory lot, Victor."

Suddenly, the red door opened and a blond-haired, young woman in a plain, white gown was standing there, speaking and welcoming the old lady in. Umma stood her ground a moment, though. Again, the young woman spoke, and she stood aside, again, gesturing her into the house. This time, Umma hobbled on in, leaning a moment against the door frame. The young woman took her arm, and she flinched. A hard edge came into the young woman's eyes, and Umma stiffly kept their arms linked.

"Is this witch Nonni a blond girl with blue eyes?" Gordon asked.

"I believe so," Victor told him.

"Well then, Umma is now in her house."

"How interesting."

"It seems more sad than interesting to me," asserted Gordon.

"Perhaps," Victor agreed, "but interesting, nonetheless."

Gordon merely grunted, too fascinated by what he saw to keep talking. Umma was now in Nonni's parlor. It was a pleasant room, with comfortable chairs, artwork and mirrors adorning the walls, sunlight streaming in through one window, and tea and biscuits sitting on elegant trays on a short table in front of her. She sat on a couch and looked around the room once or twice then directed her gaze at her lap where her hands fidgeted nervously with a bit of loose fabric from her shawl.

Nonni offered her a biscuit and a cup of tea, which she accepted with trembling hands. Nonni sat in a tall chair across the table from her, legs crossed, arms resting on the carved arms of the chair. The arms of the chair ended in carven wolves' heads whose eyes were painted red, and whose tongues stuck out, forked like those of serpents.

They talked. Gordon tried very hard to read Nonni's lips, but could not. She appeared gracious enough, but also seemed to be speaking very firmly.

"I'd give a lot to hear what the witch is saying," Gordon told Victor.

"What are they doing?"

"They're sitting in Nonni's parlor eating biscuits, drinking tea, and talking."

"That's certainly innocuous enough."

"But why is she there?"

Finally, Nonni rose, stepped over to Umma and offered her arm again. Tentatively, Umma put her hand on Nonni's pale arm and rose. Nonni led her over to one of the mirrors. The old woman regarded the mirror, her eyes shifting focus between her reflection and the fresh, lovely reflection of the witch. The witch was speaking in her ear. Gradually, her eyes rested only on her own reflection, and, gradually, the reflection changed. The hair grew darker, the wrinkles grew less deeply indented in her skin. The color of her skin became less weathered. Amazed, Gordon related this information to Victor.

"Tucker is recording for you, Sir Gordon, so keep telling us what you see."

"When did Tucker get here?"

"Several minutes ago, good man. He moved softly, so as not to disturb you."

The old woman was now become quite young in the mirror. She could have been the age of Nonni, who smiled triumphantly beside her. Her hair was blond and long and straight. Her eyes were bright in her smoothed-out, younger face. She was tan - after all, she was a peasant - but she was not age spotted, and her skin had a healthy cast to it. Her hands had come up to her face as the change took place, and now she looked at them. Though her reflection was young, her hands, before her, were still old, and she turned from the mirror, wetting those hands with her tears.

Nonni caught those wet, old hands and pulled them down so the old woman was looking in Nonni's bright eyes. For some time, Nonni spoke to her. The old woman shook her head at first, but Nonni kept speaking to her. At last, the old woman nodded her head, agreeing, Gordon surmised.

Nonni led her back to the couch and sat her down. She watched as Nonni went into another room. She leaned over to see through the doorway that Nonni had entered and saw it was a room with a cauldron, over which Nonni began to work. She leaned back on the couch, her hands in her lap, fidgeting again with the loose cloth from her shawl. Suddenly, she rose, tottering, and started toward the door, but then, where there had been nothing before, there was a black cat on the floor in front of her, staring up solemnly with golden eyes. The old woman stumbled backward in fright and fell onto the couch. The cat leapt onto the table and sat upon it, wrapping its long tail around its feet, its golden eyes fixedly staring at her. She sat stock still, avoiding that steady gaze.

"Nonni is working over her cauldron, and Umma is being held captive by a black cat," Gordon reported to Victor and Tucker.

"Her familiar demon, I assume," Victor said.

"If so much is known about this witch," Gordon asked, "why has no one hunted her down and burned her?"

"Her house is never in the same place twice, so far as anyone can tell."

"Hm, witches. They may be worse than vampires."

"I don't know, but they cause their own brand of mischief. I do wish that you could hear as well as see, Sir Gordon. It would help us greatly if we knew why the old woman went and what sort of bargain she has struck with the witch. I rather think that she has regretted it already."

"It seems that way. Let us hope she does no harm."

"Remember, whatever has happened has happened. The old woman is dead now."

"True enough," said Gordon, sighing. He added, "Witches aren't my focus, but I shall report what I know of this Nonni to another of your king's enforcers, I think."

"There is wisdom in that," agreed Victor, "A magician might find the witch's house using the description of its interior."

It was not too long, really, though it seemed interminable, before Nonni returned. She carried elegantly in her right hand a steaming cup. She again

31

offered her arm to Umma, who took it with a shaking hand. They went again to the mirror, and Nonni gave her the cup. She held it, not drinking it for some time. Finally, with no sign of impatience, the witch leaned close and said something in her ear. A look of desperate yearning overcame her image in the mirror, and, with Gordon silently begging her not to do it, she raised the cup to her lips and slowly drained the whole, steaming potion.

"Oh, my," said Victor when he heard this.

It must have been painful, for she fell to spasms at once, dropping the cup and staggering. She would have collapsed had Nonni not been supporting her. The witch held her up, supporting her under both arms now, standing behind her, showing her the mirror. She writhed in the witch's arms, but Nonni slipped her hands under her arms and grabbed her head and made her look. Her white hair fell out, drifting to the floor. Her skin dried out, cracked, and shook off, also drifting to the floor. Her knobby joints shrank. Her crooked bones grew straight. New hair, stuff so blond it was like spun gold, sprouted from her scalp, taut, like pins and gradually curved as it lengthened, until it fell down to her elbows. Her new skin was soft and smooth and tan. But her mouth was open as though she were screaming through it all. Finally, it was over. Amazed, she struggled to be free of the witch's embrace, and Nonni let go of her. She stood before the mirror, looking back and forth from her own form to her reflection. It was real. Her hands in the mirror and hands on her wrists matched. Her face was unwrinkled under the touch of her perfect hands. She stared for a time

32

before Nonni stepped in again, talking to her.

Gordon felt a terrible frustration at not being able to hear what had been said. Nonni gave her different clothes, the skirt and smock and shawl of a younger girl and better shoes as well. Gordon noted that these were the clothes she had died in. Nonni also gave her a sheathed knife, which she stuck into the sash around the top of her skirt. With that, and some more frustratingly silent talking, she was sent away.

# Chapter 4

It was still afternoon, and she ran, actually ran, down the path back toward the road, but when she got close, still under the shadow of the trees, she saw that Ponto was yet there, standing where the path met the road and waiting. After a moment of hand-wringing, she struck out through the woods. It took a while for her to make her way through. She was not wood crafty, and, several times, she stopped and turned in circles, looking around before she proceeded on.

Eventually, she came out of the woods and was back on the road. She walked for some time, fiddling with and often looking down at the knife tucked into skirt and hidden under her sash.

"She must have been required to kill someone in return for her youth," speculated Victor, "and she must not have done so, for she was old when she died."

"Or, she has asked to be youthful and strong for long enough to get her revenge on someone," suggested Gordon.

"I suppose we shall see,"

Another voice, Tucker's, unless there was now someone else in the room, added, "Who knows what her errand may be? Why suggest an evil intent, when you can believe the best?"

Gordon responded, "Because I gave up on being naïve long ago."

Victor added, "There's a fellow living in that village, a man named, Charles, if I'm not mistaken, who is rumored to have had some sort of relationship with Nonni in the past. Perhaps the rumor is true and has bearing on the events that unfolded last night."

"Rumors, Victor, that's all," said Tucker.

"Sir Gordon will see what he sees," said Victor.

It was not much further to the next village, and Umma was soon approaching it. Like all villages in these parts, it was walled and gated. She entered blithely through the simple gate and went to the village green before the house of the mayor and the local shrine. The wedding festivities had already commenced, and young people were dancing on the green. Musicians were playing beyond them. Mature men and women and children under their direction were making preparations upon the village green for the wedding feast to take place after the ceremony. The eyes were searching among the revelers now focusing on one face then another, all young men. They finally settled on one, blond-haired youth.

"My word," said Gordon, "I think she's infatuated with a boy."

"Is that all?" asked Victor, but after a moment he added, "Well, the heart does sometimes move even the aged to desperate actions."

"Ha! You'd know, wouldn't you?" said Tucker, "The way you make a fool of yourself over Mildred the mayor's daughter every time she's in eyesight."

There was an uncomfortable huffing from Victor, and Tucker began to laugh.

Victor said, "However fond I may be of the girl, in an avuncular fashion, I'd never go to a witch for aid in wooing her."

"Avuncular?" laughed Tucker.

35

"Gentlemen!" said Gordon, "Your talk is very distracting to me."

There was silence from them for a time, broken only by Tucker's occasional, soft snorts of amusement.

Umma was among the young revelers. She approached the blond youth and caught his eyes. He smiled at her. She moved past him casting occasional glances behind. He watched, and he followed. Soon, they were dancing together and, he was talking to her. Gordon felt certain that it was love talk, sweet wooing, and such. He was grateful not to have to hear it. Full night was about them now. The moon and stars were shining. They danced for an hour or two into the night, pausing now and then for refreshment of beer or cheap wine. Umma must have been having a grand time. She changed partners occasionally, always returning to the blond boy she had so carefully sought out. She even danced once each with the other three men who'd left her village with her that afternoon. Gordon thought they must not have recognized her at all. Of her son, there was no sign. But eventually, the pre-wedding fun ended, and the dancing was paused, for the ceremony started.

Umma slipped away from the blond boy at that point and spent a bit of time skirting about the edge of the scene. Again, she was searching faces. This time, her eyes settled upon a more mature man, a brown-haired fellow whom Gordon estimated was about thirty years old. He was standing at the edge of the green in the shadows. He had not participated in the dancing and drinking, and he hardly seemed to be there for the wedding at all, though in such affairs, usually no one in a village was omitted. Indeed, the entire village must have been there, and many from nearby villages besides.

Umma came up to him, stood close, and seemed to engage him in a quiet conversation. He gave her long, longing looks and after a short time, they walked away from the wedding, hand in hand. They stole away, (that was the only way Gordon could describe it) to a house, surely belonging to the man. Umma let him have kisses and plied him with wine while he tried to entice her into his bed. His efforts grew fumbling, clumsier and clumsier until he finally passed out. It had been some time by then already.

He lay on the floor at her feet, as ugly and pathetic as any drunk man could appear, his looks ruined by the stupor of his expression, the drool running from his mouth onto the hard packed clay of his floor. She knelt beside him and took the knife from her sash. She put its point to his chest over his heart, seized it with both hands, and raised it high. But she did not strike. With trembling hands, she lowered the knife and backed away on her knees. Gordon could guess that she was arguing with herself, working herself up to do or not do the deed.

Perhaps half an hour passed this way, and Gordon grew more and more impatient.

"As I said," Victor reminded him, "the vision takes as long to see as it took to live."

"Well, damnit, why doesn't she just leave if she's not going to kill him as Nonni requires?"

"The formation of conscience can be a difficult thing," said Tucker, "have you never argued with yourself?"

"I'm not concerned with her problems," snapped

Gordon, "but with the identity of her killer."

"All in due time, Sir Gordon," said Victor.

Suddenly, Gordon saw not the poorly lit room where Umma knelt near the comatose body of the man she was required to kill, but the bright, blond face of the boy she had spent so much time with dancing on the village green. Then, he saw her hands speed up and down, plunging the point and blade of the knife deeply into the man's chest.

"Good God, she's killed him!" said Gordon finding that he was regaining sensations in his limbs and could move his hands. He heard exclamations from both Victor and Tucker.

She fell back from the body immediately, scrambling across the room. She stared at it for several minutes with her arms wrapped around her legs.

"I don't understand," said Gordon, "she saw someone who wasn't there, she saw that blond boy for just an instant before she stabbed."

"Yes, yes," said Victor, "sometimes one sees not what is there before one but what one wants to see. Has this never happened to you?"

"No," said Gordon, "my eyes see whatever is before me."

"Perhaps you are a fortunate man for that, but many a man has seen with his eyes not what is before his eyes but before his heart."

"I feel obliged to believe it. There, she's getting up now. She's washing her hands in a basin. She's a frightened murderer, that's certain. Her hands are trembling. She weeps."

Umma washed her face as well and dried her hands

38

and face on her skirt.  She hastily fled the house, leaving the knife plunged into the chest of her victim.  Gordon watched as she returned to the wedding, mixed in among the guests, and sought, frantically he thought, the blond boy.  They found each other soon, for he appeared to have been searching for her as well.  She took him by the hand and led him first to the beer and then to the dance ground.

Gordon said, "Tucker, you spoke of conscience, but here she is reveling in her reward, rejoicing with the boy. It was not conscience she was building up but courage for a cowardly act."

Tucker made no response.

Victor said, "That being settled, we can at least send word, relating the fate of the man to his kin."

"At least," said Gordon.

He found himself telling them less and less of the vision as it progressed, and they prompted him less and less, simply awaiting the attack of the vampire.  Umma romanced the boy, taking him aside to a barn after many dances and much beer and wine.  In the hay they embraced and kissed.  Just as Gordon was beginning to find it very uncomfortable and wishing he would not have to witness their fornication, they abruptly stopped.  The boy stood up as if listening then hastily dressed.  Umma followed suit, following at his heals when he jogged back to the village green.  They arrived on a scene quite different from the one from which they had snuck away. The festivities were halted and a crowd had gathered around something in the middle of the green.  The boy took Umma by the hand and led her through the crowd toward the front.  At length, they found themselves able to peer through to see what the apparent hubbub was about. Laid out on blankets, and being attended by some village women, was the brown-haired man with the dagger yet sticking out of his chest. He was moving a little, and despite the evident concern on peoples' faces, it was clear that he would likely live. The wound had not been made with skill, and she had evidently missed any vital parts.

Umma pulled away from the blond boy and covered her face with her hands. Turning quickly from the scene, she pushed back through the crowd to get clear, to get away. She shoved, scrambled, and tripped her way through, and when she was clear, she ran. If she was followed, she was not caught up with. She made it out through the village gate, leaving it open behind her. Downhill she went, down the road into the dark with no light to guide her feet. She tripped up often, but rose each time and continued to flee. Eventually, she turned and saw that the lights of the village were no longer visible, and then she simply fell to the ground. Gordon supposed she was weeping. And this went on for an amount of time he could only find to be interminable.

"Patience," advised Victor, "it will end, my friend."

"No doubt," said Gordon, refraining from spouting the foul curses he felt boiling up on the tip of his tongue.

# Chapter 5

In the dark, Jack, Robert, and Christopher found her, presumably from the sound of her weeping. They helped her up and led her on toward home, lighting their way with torches. Gordon wished he could hear what pathetic excuse she offered for her circumstances. He surmised that in the dark, failing to keep her part of the bargain, she had become old again. As her eyes swept briefly at the night sky, he saw by the stars that it was close to dawn. Along the road, they intersected with the path leading off to Nonni's house, and there they found Ponto. He aided her steps, and they hurried on in the dark to the village.

"Oh, they're close!" exclaimed Gordon, "close. It'll be any moment now." He was beginning to tremble with excitement.

They were at the bottom of the hill on which their village stood and just about to ascend. Umma had stopped wiping periodically at her face and was leaning very heavily on Ponto's arm. Her eyes were gazing at the ground seeking her next step, and so she missed the entrance of the vampire completely. They stopped only a few yards up the road, and she belatedly looked up ahead. Standing in the middle of the path was the figure of a man. He was just outside the circle of light from their torches, and the torches atop the village gate backlit him distantly.

"The vampire has made his appearance," said Gordon, straining against the ties securing him to the chair as if he could move to make a difference in the day old scene he was witnessing.

"Is it the one you seek?"

"I can't tell. She couldn't see him clearly. I think he's talking to them."

The boy, Jack, went up toward the dark figure in a friendly fashion, holding his torch high. In the torch light, the figure was revealed as very pale. It flashed its teeth, revealing long, sharp canines. Jack backed up, nearly loosing his footing on the incline. The figure threw its head back, perhaps laughing or howling. Umma turned to flee, Ponto dragging her along. One of the men, he couldn't tell if it were Robert or Christopher ran past toward the vampire and Jack. The other was running with them. Umma glanced over her shoulder in her fright, tripped, and fell causing Ponto to tumble too. She rolled onto her back, now facing uphill. The vampire was walking briskly along the road after them with Jack struggling, tucked under an arm, as he sucked blood from his neck. The other, village man, Gordon thought it was likely Christopher, was beating the vampire with the torch, but to no effect. Umma began scrambling away on the ground. Ponto lifted her by her arms and dragged her so she saw the vampire discard Jack and leap over taking Christopher by the throat with one hand. At this point Robert came back with a pointed stick in hand and tried to thrust it into the vampire's chest, but it batted him aside. He fell to the ground and struggled to rise. Christopher dropped the torch and tried to pry the vampire's clawed hand away from his throat. With its free hand, the vampire slapped him twice, and he went limp. It brought his neck up to its mouth and bit.

Ponto had Umma on her feet by then and put an arm

around her, helping her along. They ran from the scene, soon losing the road in the darkness, or perhaps leaving it on purpose, and stumbling along through a wheat field. It seemed to be very quickly after that the vampire found them. He parted the wheat in front of them and slashed open Ponto's belly with his claws. Umma fell, of course, but started to crawl away.

Gordon had to stop narrating when the vampire lifted her off the ground and held her before him. It was the former cooper. Her eyes could see his face faintly in the moonlight and star shine. He bit her and took a long time drinking her blood.

"Out, out!" cried Gordon, "get these eyes out of me. I've seen enough! It is Dudley the cooper."

"Don't panic, Sir Gordon," said Victor, "Be calm, I can't extract the eyes quickly, you know. It's a delicate thing to do. Just tell Tucker what you've seen while I prepare."

"You'll have to numb me again," he said.

"Yes, yes, it will have worn off by now."

There was a knock at the door.

"That'll be Sue returning. It must be nearly dawn, now," said Victor.

In Umma's vision, dimming now, no longer struggling, he guessed, the former cooper was still leisurely draining away her life. Ponto was struggling to his feet, trying to hold his guts in and pull his knife from his belt. As he rose to strike, the vampire turned casually, supporting Umma with one hand, and stuck him down again with the other. He then returned to sucking at her neck.

43

There was another knock at the door. "Go get that, Tucker. Tell her to come back in just a little bit, and we'll be all done here."

Gordon could hear Tucker rise, set aside his pen and parchment, and walk away down the hall.

"Here, drink this, Sir Gordon. I can begin the extraction as soon as you're done. I assume it will not be necessary to see through the eyes of any of the others?"

"There's no need," said Gordon, quivering with rage as he saw the face of Umma's murderer hold her eyes to his as she slowly died in his arms. He opened his mouth and drank the nondescript tasting draught that Victor carefully poured into him. Down the hall, Tucker was speaking to someone politely and a soft voice was responding in equally polite tones. Gordon couldn't make out any words.

When it was drunk down, he said, "Have you no jokes now, Victor? Distract me from what I'm seeing."

Victor chuckled.

From down the hall, Gordon heard Tucker saying pleasantly, "Yes, please come in, sir."

"Have we a guest so early?" asked Victor.

"There's a good fellow here to see you," Tucker said.

Warm contentment flowed through Gordon. His fingertips and toes began to tingle.

In the vision, Dudley the former cooper set Umma on the ground so that she could see him finish off her son with equal leisure.

"Quickly, Victor, this vision won't end, and I've never felt like a victim before. End this."

"Are you numb?"

44

"Yes," he lied.

There was a sudden, surprised sound from Tucker and a cry from Victor. Gordon was sure that he heard a body hit a wall and slide down to the floor.

"But you can't enter a God-fearing man's house," protested Victor.

"I was invited in," explained a bland voice.

"Set me free, Victor," said Gordon, but he knew it was too late for that.

There was the sound of metal piercing flesh, and of Victor crying out in pain.

"May you burn in hell," said Victor.

"Hell? Nonsense. I'm immortal," said the bland voice.

Victor cried out some more, and Gordon heard his body slump to the floor.

"I beg your patience, Sir Gordon," said the bland voice, "I must see to these tasty bits first. But here, let me take this cloth off your eyes."

# Chapter 6

The cloth was removed and Gordon had the disorienting view of see Dudley the cooper looking at him in Victor's candlelit operating room and from over the corpse of Ponto in the moonlit, wheat field. He was in the brief stage that vampires have between feedings when they look enough like other people to pass for ordinary. Smiling, he raised Gordon's head and showed him first Tucker then Victor. Tucker was in the doorway on the floor. Victor was on the floor beside Gordon's chair. The eye extractor had been shoved into his belly and out the other side.

"Don't worry," said Dudley, "He's plenty warm enough for me."

"How did you find me?" asked Gordon, feeling the numbness overtaking him now.

"You're very calm about it," said Dudley, "Quite as brave as your reputation. That's good. You shouldn't give me the satisfaction of making you plead for your life." He patted Gordon's cheek and set his head back between the restraints on either side of it.

In the vision, Umma's sight was fading out, only shadows and moonshine remained, hazy and indistinct. The lights of the candles in the present showed the scene at Victor's more pressingly. With his head between the restraints, Gordon saw only the ceiling and candles. His mouth was going numb. Beside him on the floor, he heard Dudley bite Victor and begin feasting. Impotent rage filled his mind even as the numbness came full on his body. He couldn't even spit his defiance.

Presently, Dudley rose from the floor, using the cloth that had covered Gordon's mouth to tidy up his bloody lips.

"To answer your question, I lucked upon you. I was scouting the town for my next meal, peering in windows for the choicest victims when I heard your voice. I've been listening at that window for hours. You're a singularly dull storyteller, Sir Gordon. You give no life to a tale. If it hadn't been of personal interest to me, I assure you I would have moved on. But there you were regaling me with my own exploits. I had to stay to hear my part in the story."

He reached down and wiped blood from the cloth onto Gordon's cheeks, smiled thinly and said, "You can't talk now, can you?"

Gordon stared back, hoping his eyes conveyed the contempt he felt for this monster.

"He numbed you, but he must have done something else to let you speak? Is it this?" He produced the mother-of-pearl ointment pot from the table where Victor had kept his tools. "Yes, it must be, mustn't it?"

He dipped several claws into it and rubbed Gordon's jaws with the stuff.

"I expect this will take effect soon enough. In the meantime, I must decide how to proceed. I've no interest in biting you, yet. There's still some time 'til the dawn, and I can hide in this house all day, if need be. It's quite large and there are several windowless rooms and a basement or two. I think I shall have to see if I can't give you the benefit of the other eyes. You saw the last day of the old woman. Perhaps you'd like to see the last day of the others as well. I might be able to arrange that for you, before I suck you dry." He smiled blandly at Gordon and began rummaging around the room. He bent over beside the chair, and Gordon heard him pull the eye extractor out of Victor's belly. He stood and held it up. Blood and gore dripped from it. The vampire examined it carefully. He hummed as he wiped it off with the same cloth that had covered Gordon's eyes. He wiped blood and gore into Gordon's hair as he played with the instrument.

"Sturdy," he commented, "I don't think I've made it unusable." He set it aside and started looking around for something else. On Victor's instrument table were the two enchanted bags for the eyes and the eye-connector. He fiddled with the eye-connector for a moment and said, "This must be the tool for putting a new eye in the head, yes."

Gordon was sure he could talk by that point, but saw no point in saying anything.

"And the bags must have the eyes in them," Dudley said. He opened the golden bag and looked in. He smiled a wan, tight, little smile at what he saw.

"It pleases you, then," said Gordon, "that you put the lights out in all of them?"

Dudley favored him with the same smile, "A man has to eat, Sir Gordon."

"I never tortured a cow before slaughtering it, nor any man or vampire I had to kill."

"You lack imagination," commented Dudley, picking the eye extractor up again. "I believe I understand how this works. Like so, yes?" He placed it over Gordon's left eye socket.

There was a knock at the door. Gordon drew a fast breath to shout, but faster than a shout the vampire slapped him a stunning blow across the face. He lay dazed as Dudley called out in a good imitation of Victor's voice, "Who is it?"

The muffled sound of a woman's voice carried to them, stating diffidently, "It's Sue. Are you done?"

"Yes, Sue, we're quite finished," said Dudley, pulling Tucker's body into the room.

"Is it tidy in there?" she asked.

"I'm just done tidying up, Sue," said Dudley, stuffing the bloody cloth into Gordon's mouth.

"Well then, I'll prepare some breakfast," said Sue, opening the door.

"Splendid!" declared Dudley, stepping over to the wall by the doorway so he was hidden from view. Gordon struggled to clear his head and make noise. Just as he was beginning to shout through the cloth stuffed in his mouth, Sue stopped in the hallway and stared at him in dismay.

"What," she began, but she spoke no further. Dudley stepped out swiftly and seized her by the throat, choking off further sound. He carried her in thus, one handed while she struggled to breath, grasping ineffectually at his clawed hand.

"Nicely done, Sir Gordon," Dudley said.

Gordon struggled with tongue and teeth, working his jaws desperately to get the gory cloth out of his mouth.

"Allow me," said Dudley, and whipped the cloth out fast.

"It doesn't matter," said Gordon.

"Eh, what?" asked the vampire.

"It doesn't matter if you kill me and the girl or even this whole town. Your destiny is still to swim forever in a lake of unquenchable fire that burns but does not consume."

"Oh, there, that's better, and I was just saying that you lacked imagination."

"It's not my imagination."

Dudley smiled that bland smile and continued choking Sue unconscious. Gordon watched, forcing himself to watch rather than close his/Umma's eyes. "So I don't get to kill you," he said, "It doesn't matter. You'll get cornered, staked and left out in the sun to burn by someone else."

"So I've been told before, but things just keep going my way." He relaxed his hold on Sue's neck just a little, watching carefully as she weakened and passed out.

"She's an innocent," Gordon said.

"She's a woman and probably a whore," said Dudley, "but mainly she's a suitable target for my practice attempts in removing eyes." He settled her into one of the armchairs, tilting her head back just so. Gordon began to pray out loud for her.

"Keep doing that, and I'll cut your tongue out," said the vampire.

Gordon raised his voice, reciting every word carefully, "Oh, my Jesus, forgive us our sins, save us from the fires of hell, and lead all souls into heaven, especially those most in need of your mercy. Amen. St. Michael, the Archangel, defend us in battle. Be our safeguard against the wickedness and snares of the devil."

50

Dudley turned on him, staring with livid eyes.

Gordon didn't stop but recited more loudly than before, "May God rebuke him we humbly pray, and do Thou, O Prince of the heavenly host, by the power of God, cast into hell Satan and all the evil spirits, who prowl about the world seeking the ruin of souls. Amen."

He started over, but Dudley hit him, with his fist this time, breaking teeth and cutting his lips. He was stunned again. The room swam before his/Umma's eyes.

Vaguely, he was aware of Dudley straddling Sue and using the eye-extractor on her. She moaned as she came conscious again. As he pulled out her second eye, she screamed. He stuffed the bloody cloth in her mouth.

"Well," he said, calm again, "that went properly. I do believe I can do this. You'll enjoy several more deaths before I'm done with you."

Gordon's/Umma's eyes were coming back into focus. He watched as Dudley placed Sue's blue eyes onto his fingers and waggled them a little before placing them in a pocket of Gordon's shirt. He applied pressure, presumably squishing them. Gordon, of course, could not feel it. Dudley lifted Tucker up where Gordon could see him and sank his teeth into the young man's neck. Tucker moaned slightly, but did not awaken. After several minutes of this, Dudley ripped the throat open and let the young man's body fall. He pulled the cloth out of Sue's mouth and wiped his lips with it. This time he smeared the blood onto Gordon's hands.

"I'm living proof," he said.

"Of what?" Gordon asked through his smashed mouth.

Dudley didn't answer right away. He had noticed Gordon's equipment stacked off to one side and started going through it. From her armchair, Sue was softly groaning. Gordon heard her slide off it onto the floor. He thought she was crawling away into a corner.

"The tools of your trade," Dudley said, dumping a crucifix out of the pack and kicking it out into the hall.

"Five vampires have fallen to those tools," Gordon said.

"But five only," answered the vampire. "Tell me, do you say a prayer as you hammer a stake through a vampire's chest? Is that the proper form?" He lifted two handfuls of stakes out of Gordon's pack. "What's this, Sir Gordon?" he asked, "There's actually a stake with my name on it!" A genuine tinge of excitement lit his voice.

"I'm not the only one carrying such a stake," Gordon said.

Dudley brandished it and placed it point first toward his heart. "It's very flattering to have a weapon made just for the taking of my life. I'll keep this and use it on as many of my victims as whims take me. I think I'll keep your armor and sword as well, for the same purpose."

"They won't avail you so much as you think," Gordon said.

"Why not? Is it because God is not on my side? I'm the contradiction to your prayer, Sir Gordon," he said, leaning over and gazing with his livid eyes into Umma's old eyes. "I'm the proof that it's hopeless for you. St. Michael never cast Satan and the evil spirits into hell. We're here with you all the time. God has no mercy. He didn't have mercy on me when I was bitten. He won't have mercy on you. If he hears, he does not care. I'm going to make you die as many times as I can. After that, I'm going to bite you, suck a little of your blood, kill Sue before your eyes, undo the straps that hold you down, and leave you to follow in my footsteps. It will be interesting to see how long you last against the need to drink blood before you take your first victim, Sir Gordon. In the end, you'll thank me for the truth I've shown you, and you'll revel in living it out."

Gordon swallowed hard and tore his gaze away. It was a mistake to look a vampire in the eye. He closed his eyes and tried to focus on the continuing sound of Sue's pain. He said, "To the end, I remain faithful to my God. Bite me if you will, but I'll walk out into the morning sun with prayer on my lips."

Dudley laughed a dry, little laugh. He said, "The pain of the light will drive you into Victor's cellar where you'll hide, growing thirstier and thirstier until nightfall. I give you two nights, at most, before you're biting with abandon." He showed Gordon his teeth, and Gordon looked on them.

"You're afraid, Sir Gordon," he said.

Gordon said nothing. He looked away. Dudley laughed more as he picked up the bag and began sorting through, deciding which eyes to place next in Gordon's sockets, lining them up on the instrument table. He lifted the silver bag and asked, "What special eyes are set aside in here?"

Gordon did not answer. He closed his eyelids over Umma's old eyes and sighed. Of course, he'd never have his own eyes in his head again. It made no difference.

53

He'd have to use all his strength to force himself out into the sun after he was bitten in a while.

"There're yours, aren't they," said Dudley, and he laughed again that dry, little laugh. He shook the silver bag. "My, my, bet you'd like these back in your head, wouldn't you. I think not. I think I'll eat them." Looking steadily at Gordon, he untied the draw strings and pulled the bag wide open with a quick tug. Captured rays of sunset, soft and red, lit the room, shining briefly and brightly on Dudley's chest and face. In an instant, his expression turned from that of calm conceit to transfixed panic. In another instant, the flesh and bone from his chest upwards burst into flames and charred away to ash. The silver bag fell to the floor. The partial corpse, smoking and stiff, fell forward, knocking over the instrument table and scattering its contents. The tools clattered, the eyes made soft plops, and the potion containers shattered.

# Chapter 7

Gordon was too stunned and elated for anything to register for some minutes.

Finally, he sang out, "Alleluia! Sue, can you come to the sound of my voice?"

He heard only her groaning.

"Sue, the vampire is dead. His head and shoulders are burned away. If you can come over here and follow my directions, you'll free me, and I'll give you eyes, if I can."

"Oh, God, he took my eyes out!" she cried.

"I know, Sue, but do as I say."

"I'm blind," she wailed.

"I know."

"Is it really you, or did he kill you, and now he's using your voice like he used Victor's?"

"It's me, Sue. I'm Sir Gordon, not the vampire."

"How do I know? Oh, God, stop tormenting me. Just kill me if that's what you intend."

"God is not tormenting you, nor is the vampire. Don't you smell that odor of charred flesh? He's dead I tell you. Come to the sound of my voice."

From the corner across the room, she rose, hugging the wall, staring from empty eye sockets. "Please be the knight and not the vampire," she begged.

"Just come to the sound of my voice, Sue. Step slowly and carefully; the floor is going to be slippery and there are . . . things in the way. You'll have to step over them.

With agonizing slowness, the blind maid made her way across the room. She tripped and fell over a corpse, either Tucker's or the vampire's. Gordon couldn't see which. He guided her with his voice. She came, frightened and desperate, convinced, he was sure, that he was really the vampire toying with her. At last, she found her way to him, having slipped into and crawled through blood. He was aghast to see the condition of her clothing. She clung to the chair and felt along it, finding his mouth and listening to him talk before she was convinced that he was not the vampire teasing his prey. She found the straps holding his right arm and undid them. After that, Gordon told her to hand him the ointment pot. She fumbled on the floor, crying out and flinching away when she realized she was contacting the burned off stump of Dudley's corpse. She cut herself on the shards of the broken pottery, but she picked up a fragment of the bowl that still had ointment in it and pulled herself back up to the chair.

"You'll have to rub the ointment on as much of my chest and arms as you can," he instructed. Feeling her way around, she freed his other arm and undid his shirt so she could get the ointment on him. When she was done, and the ointment had taken effect, he finished freeing himself. There wasn't sufficient ointment to cover his legs, so he had to maneuver to an armchair using his arms and leaning on Sue. Once in a chair, he surveyed the scene anew. As he had thought, the last of the batch of Victor's numbing potion was shattered and wasted on the floor. The eye connector was atop Victor's corpse, looking quite undamaged. The remaining eyeballs were scattered around the room in varying degrees of squishiness. He reckoned they were unusable.

"Get yourself into the chair, Sue," he ordered.

She felt her way into and sat back, trembling. She asked, "Are you going to put my eyes back in?"

He looked at the silver bag on the floor. If its magic worked as he understood it to work, his own eyes were secure in it. "You'll have eyes again, Sue," he assured her, "We have only to wait for the use of my legs again, or for a competent visitor to come and knock on the door."

He wondered if he could really work the eye connector. Only Victor had been competent, and it was probable that only Tucker had ever seen him use it. That Dudley had used the extractor successfully gave him some hope, but he had no desire to ever use that tool. There was no more numbing potion. He reached down, fingers just brushing the silver bag where it lay near the stake with Dudley's name on it. He stretched for it, snagged it, and pulled it up. He opened it gingerly and peered inside. By the candle light given off by the many, stubby candles still lit about the room, he saw his own eyes, apparently no worse for the wear. He shut the bag quickly. It was too unnatural. So they waited, Gordon in the armchair, Sue in the operating chair, the vampire's corpse and the corpses of the last victims he ever took laying messily on the floor, and a dim light beginning to show around the shutters of the room's only window.

"We've survived, Sue," Gordon said a little later, "we have only to wait, and all will be well."

Sue whimpered a little then said, "I'm trying to be brave, Sir Gordon, but it hurts so."

Gordon sighed in sympathy and tried to reach over to

pat her on the foot, which was the only part of her that he had any hope of reaching, but did not when it became clear that he would fall out of the chair if he pushed so hard. So they waited in silence for a time. A few rays of sunlight came through the shutters and illuminated the ceiling and the west wall.

"Do you suppose that anyone would hear us if we shouted, Sue?"

"I don't think so, Sir Gordon," she said, "That window looks out into Victor's garden, which is large and walled. These walls are thick. I could only hear Victor – I mean the vampire - from the front door by listening closely."

Gordon restrained a sigh, "No matter, all will soon be well."

There was a sudden movement in the window. The shutters moved a little to reveal a small, reptilian face squeezing between the cracks. A bright, blue snake slid its body through the crack and moved sinuously down the wall using a candle sconce and then the top of a short cabinet. It was a slender thing, some four feet long. Gordon raised the vampire stake, readying to throw it if the serpent moved to strike at him or Sue. He wondered if it were venomous or a constrictor. It slipped to the floor and slithered on across behind the operating chair. It stopped a moment, examined an eyeball still relatively fresh on the floor, opened its mouth, engulfed the thing, and swallowed it whole, root and all. Gordon shuddered. The snake flicked its tongue out at him and went on to the doorway, staying far enough away that he could not simply reach down and strike at it. It glanced back at the room, looking directly at Gordon then Sue then eased out of the room on into the interior of Victor's house.

Gordon lowered his arm and found that he was trembling. He said aloud, "In all my life, I've never felt so helpless as during this past night. Even now, I'm not much use."

"Your presence is a great comfort to me, Sir Gordon," said Sue.

"Well, that's something," he said, keeping his eye on the doorway.

"Were you scared when Victor operated on you?" she asked.

"I was nervous, though I hardly had time to think about it. He was very distracting."

"So I've heard," she said.

"How often did he perform such operations?"

"Only a few times a year. I never stayed around to witness it. He had Tucker to do all for him when he operated. Oh poor Victor, poor Tucker. They were good men, Sir Gordon." The grief in her voice made him swallow hard.

"So they seemed to me," he said, "It is a bad enough thing to lose any good man, but doubly so to lose men of such rare skills as these two possessed."

He kept his eyes on the doorway as they talked, listening for any sound at all, though the snake had moved almost noiselessly.

He asked her, "Then he never had another assistant? He was training no one else?"

"No, no one."

"Did he write down his recipes for his potions and ointments?"

"I don't think so."

59

# Chapter 8

Gordon wasn't sure if she simply appeared in the doorway, or if he had looked away a moment, and she had stepped into the room then, but suddenly the witch, Nonni, robed in blue that matched her eyes, her hair done up like a queen's, was in the doorway to the operating room. He caught his breath from the twin shocks of her presence and the effect of her incredible beauty. Somehow, she was far more radiant and appealing than she had been in Umma's vision.

"What's the matter?" asked Sue.

He swallowed hard, his mouth suddenly dry, and croaked, "We have a visitor."

"Oh, thank the Lord!" she said, "Help us. I have no eyes and Sir Gordon cannot walk."

Nonni looked quietly on them, her eyes a mystery, her mouth almost smiling, almost pensive. After a moment's silence, Sue asked, "Who is it? Sir Gordon, you did say someone had come to help."

He found his voice again, "I don't know if she is here to help, Sue. Our guest is the witch, Nonni." He was carefully neutral in tone, and he kept the vampire stake in his hand ready to wield, however impotent his position felt. Sue let out a low moan and sat up, her hands out, warding.

"You have nothing to fear from me, Sue," said Nonni in a musical voice.

That voice was exactly as Gordon had imagined it to be, the voice of a lover. He shook his head and dragged his eyes away from her face. He focused on the possible threat. She had not in any way emphasized that it was only Sue who had nothing to fear, but still, she had been speaking only to Sue.

"What do you want?" asked Sue, clearly afraid, but with a hint of defiance in her voice.

"I have come to help you. That is what I do."

"You help?" said Sue, "I know the stories about you. Your home village was overrun with rats and everyone died of the plague after they angered you."

"Dear, child," said the witch, "plagues happen in the absence of witches as often as not. I grieved for my kith and kin. I would have helped them, if only they would have accepted me."

"Why do you sound like her?" asked Sue.

"Like who, dear child?"

"You sound like my sister."

"I'm often told that I remind people of those they love. It means nothing but what you make of it. Coincidence."

Gordon found his voice again, "And what do you want with me, Nonni?"

She walked, floated it seemed, though her feet touched the floor, to his chair and touched his shoulder, "Friendship, sir knight. I desire your friendship." But her touch, her voice, her eyes, offered so much more.

"Was it friendship that you offered to Umma?" he asked through parched lips. She smiled radiantly. His mind wandered, and his memory filled with cobwebs. He desperately looked away from her. That helped. She laughed a soft, warm laugh.

"Yes, it was friendship," she said.

61

"So that's what friends do," he said, "they kill former lovers for one another?"

She reached over and touched his face with one hand, saying, "I like you, Sir Gordon. I like a strong-minded man." She gently directed his face back toward hers, with one finger under his chin, one soft, cool, caressing finger. "I know that you desire my friendship," she said.

She was awakening in him stronger desires than mere friendship, but what he said was, "I'm afraid that you are incorrect. Why don't you just be direct about your purpose?"

"Both you and Sue want your own eyes in your heads. I can do that."

"Oh, God be praised if that's all you want to do," said Sue.

"You offer this as a gift?" Gordon asked, his skepticism thick.

"I offer it to two people in need. That is all. How you show your gratitude is up to you, but ingratitude is, of course, very distasteful to me."

"My gratitude," said Gordon, "is only for your offer. We don't actually require your help. When I can stand on my own in a few hours, I'll be able to set all to right."

"Yes," said Sue, "your offer is kind, but we are not actually in need, and it would be unkind of us to accept a favor we don't really need." Gordon looked past Nonni at Sue for the space of a breath, grateful for the poor girl's support, and astonished at her resilience. She was obviously in great pain.

"Don't be silly," said Nonni, "I'm already here. I might as well assist you."

Growing impatient, Gordon said, "Just name your damnable price so we can refuse it once and for all, because I can tell you now that no amount of gratitude on my part is going to prevent me from telling the witch hunters all I know of you."

Nonni's face showed anger for only a heartbeat, "Even if I do what you cannot, give each of you his own eyes, you will still tell them all that Umma saw? What am I to you? I'm no vampire. What of the lover who spurned me? Can you truly condemn me when you don't know his crime?"

"Aside from spurning you, which would move any woman to some extreme of emotion, what did he do? Rape? Murder? Theft? Lies?"

"It was nothing you could ever understand," she said, her face a mask of mystery.

"A moment ago, you pled for my understanding. Now you insist that I can't understand. Stop playing games."

"The man is nothing to you, and furthermore, he yet lives. Let me help you, and you consider my crime amended by that act."

"No, you're no vampire, but neither are you a judge or executioner. You certainly tried to be those, though. It was only fortuitous for your Charles that he lived, so the serious degree of your crime is the same. You murdered him in your heart. Furthermore, it was a cowardly act to make Umma an assassin. Why didn't you just kill your Charles yourself?"

She laughed, and it was a proud laugh, a less beautiful laugh than ever should have come from such lips, such a throat. She stepped out of arm's reach of him, drew herself up, and said, "I'm a hunted woman, Sir Gordon. I sent Umma in fair trade, favor for favor. I sent my cat to observe. I cannot leave my woods or even my house without inviting danger. Even now, the witch hunters know that I am out of my house, out of my woods, and they search for me. When my cat told me that Umma had failed, I grieved for her, but a bargain is a bargain. When he told me of her death, I grieved the more. But, when he told me that the eye man had come to assist a vampire hunter, I was forced to take action. When I saw that the vampire was upon you, I thought I might be spared, but alas, he was a fool and was destroyed. Again, I was forced to take action. That I have taken the time to try and preserve your lives is more than you deserve. You should already be dead, and I should already be flying home before the witch hunters get close. They are about. I can feel them probing, even now."

"Fly then, before they arrive. I won't be made your servant as Umma was. Neither of us is of any use to you."

"I'll make one last attempt to bargain with you, fool," she said, and she was as stern and fierce as she had previously been charming, and no less beautiful, "I'll spare your life if you give me Umma's memories."

"Even if I felt inclined to do so, I have no idea how accomplish such a thing."

"Leave that to me," Nonni said.

"Voluntarily put myself under your power? I don't think I'll do that. I'd rather die."

"The choice is yours, Sir Gordon. I will kill you to

prevent Umma's last day from belonging to the witch hunters."

Using only the power in his tired arms, Gordon shoved himself forward thrusting the vampire stake at Nonni's breast, to pierce her heart. She stepped aside, and he fell to the floor across Tucker's bloody corpse, the stake still firmly, ineffectually in hand. Sue began to shout and flail about. Nonni stood over him, her wrath blazing forth. Out of the air, she seized a spear of ice with both hands. Gordon tried to roll away, but only his torso would move, and he didn't make it off of Tucker's corpse. Nonni plunged the spear down, but lurched suddenly forward, falling over Gordon, and stabbing the spear of ice into the floor. Gordon stabbed the stake upward, and it entered her under her ribcage. She cried out, and he found it strange that she sounded so young and girlish and so surprised, even in her agony. There was the sound of a cat yowling in hate and scratching at the shutters, which began to splinter. He thrust the stake further up and in, behind her ribs, and was sure that he pierced her heart. She lay across him a moment then rolled away onto her back, half under the operating chair. He let go of the stake and left it buried in her heart. The cat howled in anguish, and the shutters began to give in, and he realized that he needed a weapon and began trying to reach for another stake.

He stopped when Nonni looked at him with a strange, desperate look then said in fading breaths, "He would not give me a child." She went limp, and there was a puff of fire and smoke in the window as the shutters burst inward. A smell of burned hair filled the room, but no cat was to be seen.

"Sir Gordon?" Sue called out, trying to set her feet on the floor, "Oh, God help us, Sir Gordon? Did it make it in, or is it gone? Did I kick you or the witch? Who just died? Please tell me. I heard it. I heard someone dying. Where's that cat? Where's that cat?"

Gordon swallowed hard and said, "The demon familiar went back to hell, I suppose. Nonni is dead. She fell across me, and I stabbed her in the heart."

"Oh, I can't take it, Sir Gordon. I can't take it"

"It's over, Sue. There are no more enemy players in this game. Besides, you have no choice but to take it."

She bit her lip, and started to move. He pushed himself up on his arms. She felt about with her feet, stopping when she bumped Victor's corpse. "Is that you?" she asked, shakily.

"No, I'm over here. Just sit back down."

"How will you get up?"

"I'll drag myself with my arms."

"No, I'll help you."

She kept feeling around until she stepped over Victor. He told her where to step, and she made her way to him. Together, they got him back into the armchair. She sat down in his lap then, and he held onto her, stroking her hair quietly as they prayed together. They endured there at the scene of the murders until mid-afternoon when the eye-man's potion wore off, and Gordon could use his legs again.